GRANNY BLOOMERS

WRITTEN AND ILLUSTRATED BY PAULA VAUGHAN

LEISURE ARTS, INC.
Little Rock, Arkansas

Dedicated to my friend, Mary Ruth, and to my granddaughter, Annie, both of whom inspired this book and served as the models in body and spirit.

I would like to thank all of my good friends at Leisure Arts for their continued support, and a very special thank you to Tammi Williamson Bradley for taking my story and bringing it to life.

 First edition 2000

Library of Congress Cataloging-in-Publication Data
Vaughan, Paula.
Granny Bloomers / story and illustrations by Paula Vaughan.—1st ed.
p. cm.
Summary: Annie enjoys many activities with her grandmother, including gardening, catching frogs, playing dress-up, and telling bedtime stories.
ISBN 1-57486-222-7 (alk. paper)
[1. Grandmothers—Fiction] I. Title.
PZ7.V4523 Gr 2000
[E]—dc21 00-012799

10 9 8 7 6 5 4 3 2 1

Printed in Mexico

This book was typeset in Bookman Old Style.
The illustrations were painted in oil.

Leisure Arts, Inc.
5701 Ranch Drive
Little Rock, Arkansas 72223-9633

Hi, my name is Annie.

Granny Bloomers and I have been very best friends for as long as I can remember. I live in a little cottage down the road a piece from her big Victorian house. That's a good thing, since I like to visit her every day.

Granny's hair is as soft and white as cotton. She always smells like the dusting powder Mama puts on me when I get out of my bath. Granny says her wrinkles are "character lines" that come from getting old. "How old are you, Granny Bloomers?" I asked one day. "My bones are seventy, Annie," she answered with a wink, "but I'm not nearly as old as they are!"

Of all the places on earth, Granny Bloomers loves her garden the most. The animals like her garden, too. I think it's because they like to play in the sunshine near her sweet-smelling roses.

Granny's garden is the perfect place to play hide and seek. *"One, two, three, four ... Ready or not, here I come!"* Sometimes I peek so I can watch her pick up her skirt and run. I laugh because she always shows her long white bloomers. That's how she got her name.

After we finish playing, I like to walk in the garden with Granny looking at her prize roses. The neighbors are always saying, "Well, I declare, Granny Bloomers, you sure do have a green thumb!" But I see her hands all the time, and they don't look green to me. They're soft – just like rose petals.

R*rribbittt ... Rrribbittt ... Rrribbittt ...* "The frogs are sure singing today," Granny Bloomers said one morning. "Let's walk down to the pond and see what's hopping!"

In the middle of the pond sat a big green frog sunning himself on a lily pad. He and his friends were loudly croaking their frog song, *Rrribbittt ... Rrribbittt ... Rrribbittt* ... "Let's catch one!" said Granny, as she hiked up her skirt and waded through the squishy mud into the cool water. "Mama said frogs'll give you warts," I told her. But Granny just laughed and said that was an old wives' tale. I wonder ... who are those old wives and how long are their tails?

"Granny, there's nothing fun to do when it's raining," I said. I was feeling kind of grumpy.

"Nonsense," she answered. "As long as we have our imaginations, we can always find an adventure. Come with me." Then she took my hand and led me up the stairs. Granny's attic has lots of old things, with trunks full of funny-looking clothes and pictures of people I never met. Memories and men's toes. "Mementos," she corrects me. "Now let's pretend we're getting all dressed up for a party." In long dresses and floppy hats, we let the fun begin.

In her most dramatic Southern drawl, Granny said, "Why, Miss Annie, I do believe you are pretty enough to make my roses blush."

"Thank you ever so much, Miss Granny Bloomers," I offered in return. "It was so kind of you to invite me to your lovely tea party."

After a few minutes, we gave in to the giggles. Granny said she couldn't remember anything she enjoys more than playing dress-up with me.

"Is *today* the day?" I asked one morning. I was so excited. It was beautiful outside, and Granny Bloomers and I had been waiting eagerly for just the right time to observe our yearly celebration, *Annie and Granny's Great Spring Dance of Joy!*

"I do believe so, Annie," she answered. I could tell she was excited, too.

Outside, the jonquils beamed a sunny hello and cherry blossoms perfumed the air. We took off our shoes and danced barefoot in circles.

"To every thing there is a season," Granny recited, *"and a time to every purpose under heaven."* With that she lifted her hands in thanksgiving, and I followed her every move.

"April showers bring May flowers," Granny Bloomers said one day after a morning rain. She was right; our little hillside was covered with pretty blossoms. As we walked through the still damp grass, bees and butterflies danced from flower to flower, gathering nectar. "Annie, there's beauty in all things — great and small," she reminded me. Then she braided a garland of daisies for my hair.

We passed that lazy day sitting on the side of the hill and looking for cloud pictures in the sky. I even thought I saw Granny and me floating by.

Our house is always filled with excitement on Granny's birthday. We have a big party. It's lots of fun because everyone brings Granny Bloomers so many presents. Mama bakes the most delicious cake with fluffy pink icing. She lets me put the candles on the cake, and I help Granny Bloomers blow them out. "I can't wait till I have this many candles on my cake," I told her. "Well, Annie," she replied, "maybe I'll just start giving all my birthdays to you since you're in such a hurry to grow up!"

To GRANNY
BLOOMERS
From POLLY

Granny Bloomers likes to climb trees almost as much as I do. Mama and Papa worry that she might fall. They say she's getting too old to be climbing so high off the ground, but Granny says how else are you going to see how the baby birds are coming along. "Don't ever touch the babies or the nest," she whispered to me. "Their mama wouldn't like that. She's very protective of her babies, just like your mama is about you." But I'm sure glad my mama doesn't feed me worms!

Some days, with all the fun things there are for us to do, it's hard to get all of our chores done. We have to milk Granny's old brown cow, Bessie. And put the sheep out to pasture. Our favorite chore is feeding the chickens. *"Here chick, chick, chick ... Here chick, chick, chick ..."* I like saying that. In no time, the baby chicks come running to greet us with their tiny *Cheep, cheep, cheep.* They're soft and fluffy, and it tickles when I touch them.

Mr. Rosebud, Granny's old cat, always goes down to the pond with us when we go fishing. But he won't get in our boat. He doesn't like to get wet. He stays on the bank instead, keeping the birds away from our worm bucket.

"Will you bait my hook, Granny Bloomers?" She wrinkles her nose and says, "Let me see your hook, sweetie." I can tell she doesn't like this part of fishing. I guess the worms don't like it much either. "Ick, ick, ick, these are the slimiest, squiggliest, wiggle worms I've ever seen!" she tells me. I try not to laugh, but she looks so funny.

LOLLIPOP

When I spend the night with Granny Bloomers, she always starts my bedtime stories with, "Once upon a time, there was a beautiful princess named Annie ..." What a sight it is to see Granny pretending to be a fairy godmother waving a magic wand.

After the story, we go to the window and look at the stars. "If you make-believe you're connecting the dots, Annie, you can find pictures in the stars, just like in the clouds," she says softly. Sometimes we can even see the Man in the Moon.

The Prince

Before we go to sleep, Granny always reads her Bible to me. She says this old world sure would be a better place if everybody would love each other the way the Good Book says we should. When we say our prayers, I ask God to bless Mama and Papa and especially my Granny Bloomers. I can tell by Granny's prayers that she and God are real good friends.

Someday Granny Bloomers and I will have to grow up, but she will always be my very best friend.